FREEDOM BEE

a hive story by Nicole Haas

TATE PUBLISHING & Enterprises

Published by Tate Publishing & Enterprises, LLC
127 E. Trade Center Terrace | Mustang, Oklahoma 73064 USA
1.888.361.9473 | www.tatepublishing.com

Tate Publishing is committed to excellence in the publishing industry. The company reflects the philosophy established by the founders, based on Psalm 68:11,
"The Lord gave the word and great was the company of those who published it."

Published in the United States of America

ISBN: 978-1-61777-514-7
Juvenile Fiction / Social Issues / General
11.03.17

To Wyatt and Cody,
may you be forever free.

The Great Hive is famous for tumbles of honey.
Good thing, for in a bee's world, honey is money.
It shines and gleams brightly in glorious light.
While workers buzz gleefully through day and night.

Scout is a bee who worked his way to the top.
Through toil and trouble, he set up his shop.
He had come from the hive's tiniest place,
From down near the bottom, which needn't much space.

For most bees are willing to fly far from the nest,
Risking everything for themselves and the rest.
They then will produce honey back at the comb.
The busier the bee, the happier the home.

Until one day, Queen Bee in her bee buzzing voice
Said, "I'll take your pollen. I'm afraid you've no choice."
The workers grew nervous and stuttered and stammered.
The Queen had none of it. She hollered and hammered,

"Now don't be so greedy, for you must obey.
Or be banished to live far, far away.
You'll get your share do not try and dispute."
And the bees set off in troubled pursuit.

Scout worked every flower, hour after hour.
But never before had they tasted so sour.
Back at the Great Hive, Scout turned in his dough.
For a high flyin' bee, he sure did feel low.

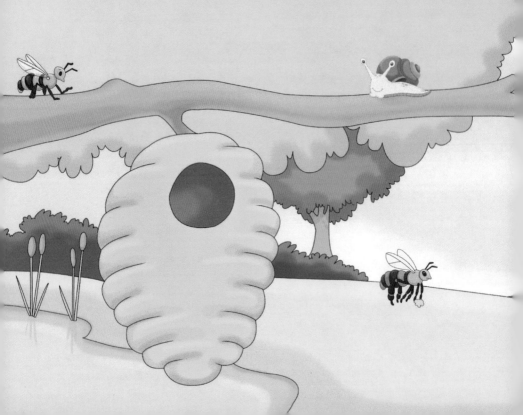

"Don't worry," said the Queen, "your needs will be met.
To depend upon me is a safe bet."
This was tough news for the self-reliant bee.
And it scraped against the grain of his liberty.

The next day he awoke to a near empty sky.
There were hardly any bees willing to fly!
Instead, in droves they slid down on the comb,
"Why should we fly and be risking to roam?"

But Scout was a worker, and work he must do.
Collecting more pollen to make golden goo.
Tired he had become as his weak bees knees shook.
The Queen took his pollen with a nervous look.

"Where'd everyone go?" Scout asked, looking 'round.

At the top of the hive, no bee could be found.

The once glowing hive looked decrepit and old.

Scout searched for the others when lo and behold...

Snap!

Down went the Great Hive to the forest floor.

The weight at the bottom it could hold no more.

In near disbelief, Scout looked down at the pile.

He then made his address to his old rank and file,

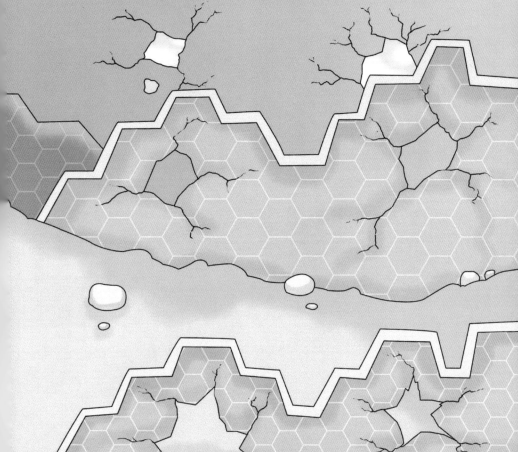

"You are all capable of much better things!
This is the moment to spread wide your wings!"
And before you could blink, they left on a whim,
To build anew from a large, leafy limb.

Together they built Great Hive number two.
Bigger and bolder, shinier and new.
It wasn't long until the Queen came calling,
"Sorry I didn't keep the Great Hive from falling."

Scout graciously stated, "Pay attention, Queen Bee,
Because, I don't work for you, but you work for me."
"Don't ever forget," said Scout. "You work for us all.
The strong and the weak, even the tired and small,

We are the workers and we make this hive hum.
For those willing to work, it's here they will come.
You have your place, and in your place you must stay
Or be prepared to be sent on your way."

And so it still is in the second Great Hive.
Bees buzzing and humming, they prosper, and thrive.
For the rest of hive time, let there never be doubt,
About the work and wisdom of the Freedom Bee, Scout.

e|LIVE

listen|imagine|view|experience

AUDIO BOOK DOWNLOAD INCLUDED WITH THIS BOOK!

In your hands you hold a complete digital entertainment package. In addition to the paper version, you receive a free download of the audio version of this book. Simply use the code listed below when visiting our website. Once downloaded to your computer, you can listen to the book through your computer's speakers, burn it to an audio CD or save the file to your portable music device (such as Apple's popular iPod) and listen on the go!

How to get your free audio book digital download:

1. Visit www.tatepublishing.com and click on the e|LIVE logo on the home page.
2. Enter the following coupon code:
   76b2-2535-28b7-d27d-d7a3-5dc9-9620-c18f
3. Download the audio book from your e|LIVE digital locker and begin enjoying your new digital entertainment package today!